2   1   3   5   7   9

4   6   8   10

ISBN 0-399-22926-4

Library of

THANKS TO AND CHARLOTTE SHEEDY AND NANCY PAULSEN FOR BEING SUPER DUPER

THANKS TO COLLEEN HALL AND ALL AT TO SARA HOROWITZ FOR MAKING THIS VERY NICE PROJECT HAPPEN.

SPECIAL THANKS TO PATRICIA RALEY AND ALL THE GRAND PEOPLE AT GRAND CENTRAL

IT'S ALWAYS
NICE TO MAKE
A GOOD
FIRST IMPRESSION

ext stop

GRAND
CENTRAL

...s Catalog Card Number 98-25135 CIP data available if you really want it but I'm sure you have better things to do. Right! G.P. Putnam's Sons I have taken trips in India and Egypt and Israel and I have never been bored because there was a some delicious character and mysterious objects and lively destination...

New York

G.P. Putnam's Sons, Reg. U.S. Pat + Tm. Off. Published simultaneously in Canada Printed in Hong Kong. So long

by
Maira Kalman

G.P. Putnam's Sons,
New York.

Dedicated
(as always)
to
T.K. LBK. and
ATDOMLK!

Singing trees.

Green birds.

The snappy new day is here. You might wake up
and play with your dog, Pete.
You might
build a chair
out of sticks,
or chew
some gum.

You might do
nothing
at
all.

But

while
you
are
sitting
there,
there is a place
in New York City that
is the busiest, fastest, biggest
place there is.
It is a train station.
This place is called
Grand Central.

One day you might (you must) go there.

It's not called grand for nothing!
Everything about it is grand! huge! monumental!
Grand staircases.
Polished marble floors.
Stupendous star-filled
ceilings.

Don't take
my picture

Every
day 500,000
people walk, run,
dash, rush—criss-crossing
on and off trains.
It is such a madhouse, people say
IT'S LIKE GRAND CENTRAL IN HERE!
How does it work?
Who does what?
What does
who?

It is 5:30 a.m.
While you are
dreaming
about a
giant
ne-eyed squid,

Lenny Maglione is
at his desk. He is
in charge of the
building. He has
316 people working
to make sure the
building doesn't
fall down. He can
see everything from
his window onto
the main concourse.

Roberto is a carpenter. He fixes doors that need to open *and* close.

Bob and Steve work the scissor lift— lifting objects heavier than a **potato** (let's say).

Ed changes one of the **kazillion** light bulbs, standing on a very tall scissor lift.

(Mel Schmeklen is just hanging around watching)

Etha delivers the mail — a letter to Mr. Pickle *cannot* go to Mr. hnikle.

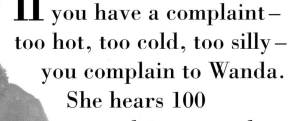

if you have a complaint— too hot, too cold, too silly— you complain to Wanda. She hears 100 complaints a week. Could you hear that many complaints and always be polite? She is.

A place has to be safe. From no-goodniks. From fires.

George Coppola
is the chief of police.
He eats a **tuna** sandwich for lunch

with Bob Hennessey,
the fire chief
(who prefers a grilled **cheese** sandwich)

Let's say twelve children  from Mamaroneck,
on their way to the Empire State Building get separated
from their teacher, Mrs. Sauerkraut.

Help!

The policemen and women and the firemen and
women will rush to their aid.
The teacher will be found. The children will be happy
(except for Arthur Beanstalk who is not crazy about Mrs. Sauerkraut).

You can't have a train station without trains. Every day 548 trains come and go.

Dave Schanoes makes sure they are on time, safe, working — not broken! Sometimes an unexpected situation happens. Then there is an emergency meeting in the Situation Room. Here is a situation:

I am not
chicken

if

you and your
best friend Gus are
on the 10:40
to Rye Playland
(yippee!!)!
and a giant chicken is on the track
blocking the train, Dave can call that chicken
and convince him logically to get off the tracks.

The Ferris wheel is waiting.

The trains work so people can work. And live.

Ethel Schloogle
is going to the
Venus Beauty Salon
for a haircut
(good luck!).

Napoleon Noble
is going to act
on Broadway.

Edith and Selma
are going to the
Metropolitan to
see a painting by
Tintoretto.

The
Oblensky
twins
are
going
to
their

tap

dancing

class

in

Carnegie
Hall.

The woman with the blue pancake hat

is going to
Chinatown
to buy
Poo Nik Tea.

Little
Ofir
Weiss i.
going
to the
Bron
Zoo.

Sidney Salmon
is going
to play
chess
with his
cousin Zoltan Zizmore.

The fezman
in the fez
is going
skating
in Central
Park.

I love
pancakes

The man in the
flat red pancake hat
is going to eat pancakes at
Joe Jr's Coffee Shop.

Pete is
on his way
to Riverdale
to cheer up
Ida Frumkiss.

Fred
Farfel is heading
to Tuckahoe
where he
will stub
his **toe**.

Mrs.
Millicent
Bluebird
is
bringing
a
rare
lemon
to
the
lemon
man
at
the
Botanical
Gardens.

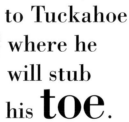

People are starting to get hungry. They race to eat. Some people say, AHOTDOGANDFRIES ANDMAKEITSNAPPY!

give me a bite please

A man
in a porkpie hat
buys cherry pies.

A woman named
Minna Fuchsbaum
says,

"This lolli pop is delicious!"

FISH IS BRAIN FOOD

Hi, New England

Hi, Manhat

At the Oyster Bar you must sit at the counter and watch Marino Marino make oyster stew. He adds 3 shakes of paprika to the stew.

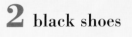

When he is not
making stew,
Marino thinks of interesting
math problems like this…

2 black shoes

+

a fish-eyed man wearing

2 black suspenders

+

an angry stickman wearing

1 black hat (with pompoms)

+

1 brown dog named Elvis

=

5 black things that

you can wear and

1 brown thing

that will bite

you if you

try to wear it

DEPARTURES
9:18 NEW HAVEN
9:20 NEW ROCHELLE
9:25 NEW BABY

I can't find my yo-yo

It's time to catch a train. If you have a question you go to Audrey in the information booth under the big clock. She can't tell you where your lost **yo-yo** is, but she can tell you where to catch the 10:27 to Valhalla, the 2:20 to Dobbs Ferry, the 4:14 to Cos Cob… but don't catch a cold!

At the ticket window you must buy a ticket (unless you are a **dog** who rides for **free**) from Robert. You can't buy a ticket to Po-DUNK, Pensi-COLA or Pe-ORIA (because these trains don't go there), but you can go to Westport, White Plains, or Williams Bridge.

 Some people travel light. With a toothbrush and a book.

Some people carry 14 suitcases, a piano, skis
and a goldfish named Leopold.
Then Melvin Johnson will help you get to the train.
He would prefer you travel light.
He does.

The trains don't drive themselves.
Mary Donch is the engineer. She puts on yellow gloves and
blue safety goggles and takes a big
brass key out of her pocket and
turns on the train. She can drive
up to 90 miles an hour. She
drives up a storm, but
safely. She can go
backwards
too.

DON'T
TICKLE
THE
ENGINEER
Thank You

GO, GO, GO, GO, GO, GO, GO

KEY

HORN

I love my fish

FISH

PAIL

DON'T EVER TOUCH THIS BUTTON →
OR SOMETHING HORRIBLE WILL HAPPEN

Thank You

BOOK

DOG

Walking
down the aisle
is the conductor.
Not of the orchestra,
of the train.
Robert takes
out his hole punch
and punches your ticket.
If you have an emergency,
like your knee itches,
tell him. He is in charge.
He will know what to do.
(Scratch it!)

This is the hole punch.
Every conductor has a different punch
with their personal punch shape.

ANDY'S PUNCH

JEFF'S PUNCH

BILL'S PUNCH

TRUDY'S PUNCH

HAWAIIAN PUNCH

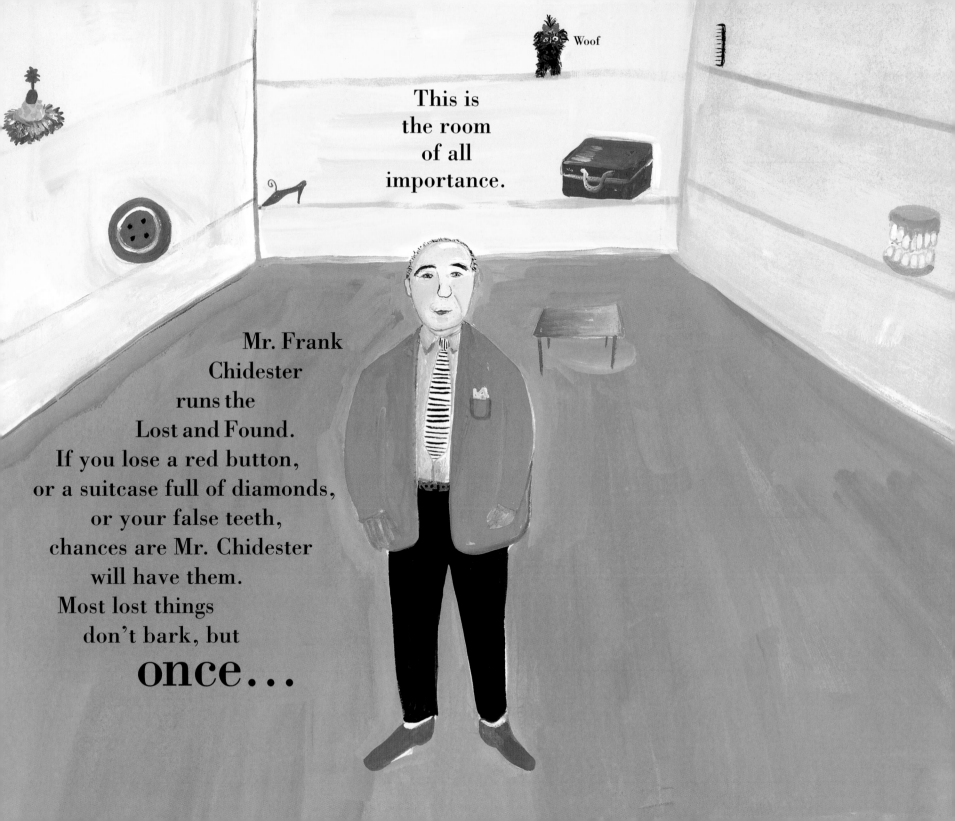

Woof

This is
the room
of all
importance.

Mr. Frank
Chidester
runs the
Lost and Found.
If you lose a red button,
or a suitcase full of diamonds,
or your false teeth,
chances are Mr. Chidester
will have them.
Most lost things
don't bark, but
once...

...once the absent minded Mrs. Clarence Pffafenburger was bringing her show dog Mitzi from Darien to Greenwich for a tea party. When Mrs. Pffafenburger got off at Greenwich, she realized to her horror that she had left Mitzi on the train.

Good bye Mitzi

But not for long.
Mr. Chidester found Mitzi
and sent her home.
On her own private train.

Things you will see in Grand Central.

Someone waiting patiently.

Someone waiting impatiently.

A very on time cloc

A peppy dog named Elv

Two triangles and a bee.

Someone looking up.

Someone looking down.

Someone sleeping.

Three gruesome gargoyles.

Someone rushing...

really rushing...

... really really rushing!!!
(it's called rush hour after all)

Things you won't see.

Boris
Pasternak
pouring
a drink for his
wife, Zinaida.

Einstein sailing.

The silver
bucket
in his dream.

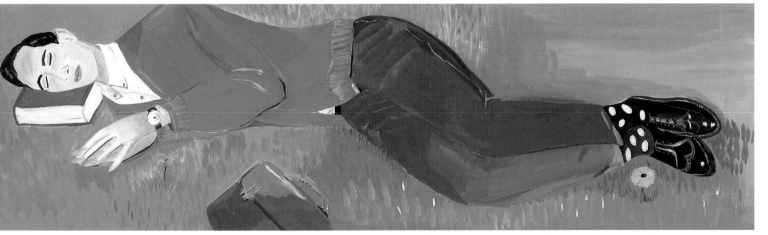

A boy named Will dreaming on a red book.

The pyramids
of Giza. (That's
another trip.)

It's 6:00 p.m. In Vanderbilt Hall…
(It was Mr. Vanderbilt who had the place
built in 1903 after all)… there is a lively celebration going on.
The singer Olga Shmedvig is
singing. When she hits her
high notes people think
it is the train whistle
and start running
for the train.

"my kneeee"

Herbert Moosehump is having fun and so is little Ervin Pil who will grow up to be a famous scientist because he eats beets every day!

this is fascinating

The place never stops,
because people work
all
night
long.

Dr. Beautyman
is going to
Roosevelt Hospital
to deliver
the Krupchik triplets
(good luck Krupchiks!).

Mel Bongo
is going to bake
600 jelly doughnuts
at Georgie's Bakery
on 125th St.

Sal Monkfish
is going home after
playing in the orchestra.

Simon LaSkunk is
going to Dover Plains to
stare at the sky.

Suki
Matsumoto
is going home
after a long
longer longest poetry
reading by Simon LaSkunk.

Zagwat Holstein is
going to his
newspaper
job.

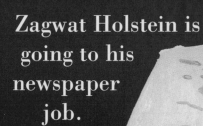

Greg is the night station master.

He has a walkie talkie.

Ralph brushes famously.

Albert sweeps swimmingly.

Great googamoogas! It's 5:30 a.m. While you are dreaming of turning your piano teacher into **a frog,** Lenny Maglione is back at work again. And that's how it goes.

Lenore protects positively.

Ed checks electricity enthusiastically.

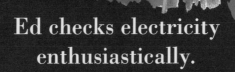

Trains are **trips.** And trips are **adventures.**

And adventures are

new ideas
and
Romance

and you can't ever know

what in the world

will happen

which is **exactly**

why

you are going.

And *kisses,*

kisses,

k i s s e s

are always there.

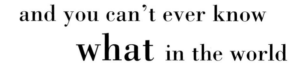

I love
you Mimi

"Hello Hello. I'm so glad to see you."

"It's been toooo long."

"You've grown **so** very **much.**"

"Good-bye."

"Good-bye."

"I love you."

"I'll miss you."

"Don't forget to write."

"Don't catch a cold."

"Be careful, darling."

"I love you."

"Good-bye."